The Three Little Hebrew Boys and the Big Bad Wolf Activity and Coloring Book; Young Writers Version © 2020 Keturah Rena
Cover Design and Illustrations by Tajha Alston
Content Editing and Interior by Keturah Rena the Affordable VA

ISBN: 978-1-951667-07-8
Published by I AM Media Books, Michigan, USA
Media to Awaken the World!

www.Iammediabooks.com

Coloring book guide

Are you ready to get creating? Are you ready to write your very own book? I'm so excited that you have chosen to go on this quest. Along the creative way, you will run into roadblocks just like I did when I wrote my story, when you hit those creative slumps know that you can push through! You might run into self-doubt, but just know that you are powerful, you are amazing, and you can accomplish anything that you set your mind to. I pray you the best of success as you create your very own 3 Little Hebrew Boys and the Big Bad wolf story, I know it will be awesome. Try your best to use good hand writing, and above all else, HAVE FUN!

Parents

It's an excellent idea to let your children first write a rough draft of their story on a separate piece of paper, which can be corrected and perfected. Once it has passed the revision phase have your child rewrite their words in the book. When they're finished, they will have their very own personalized version of The 3 Little Hebrew Boys and the Big Bad Wolf. How exciting! May the creativity flow and the fun begin. Enjoy, from my home to yours. Shalom!

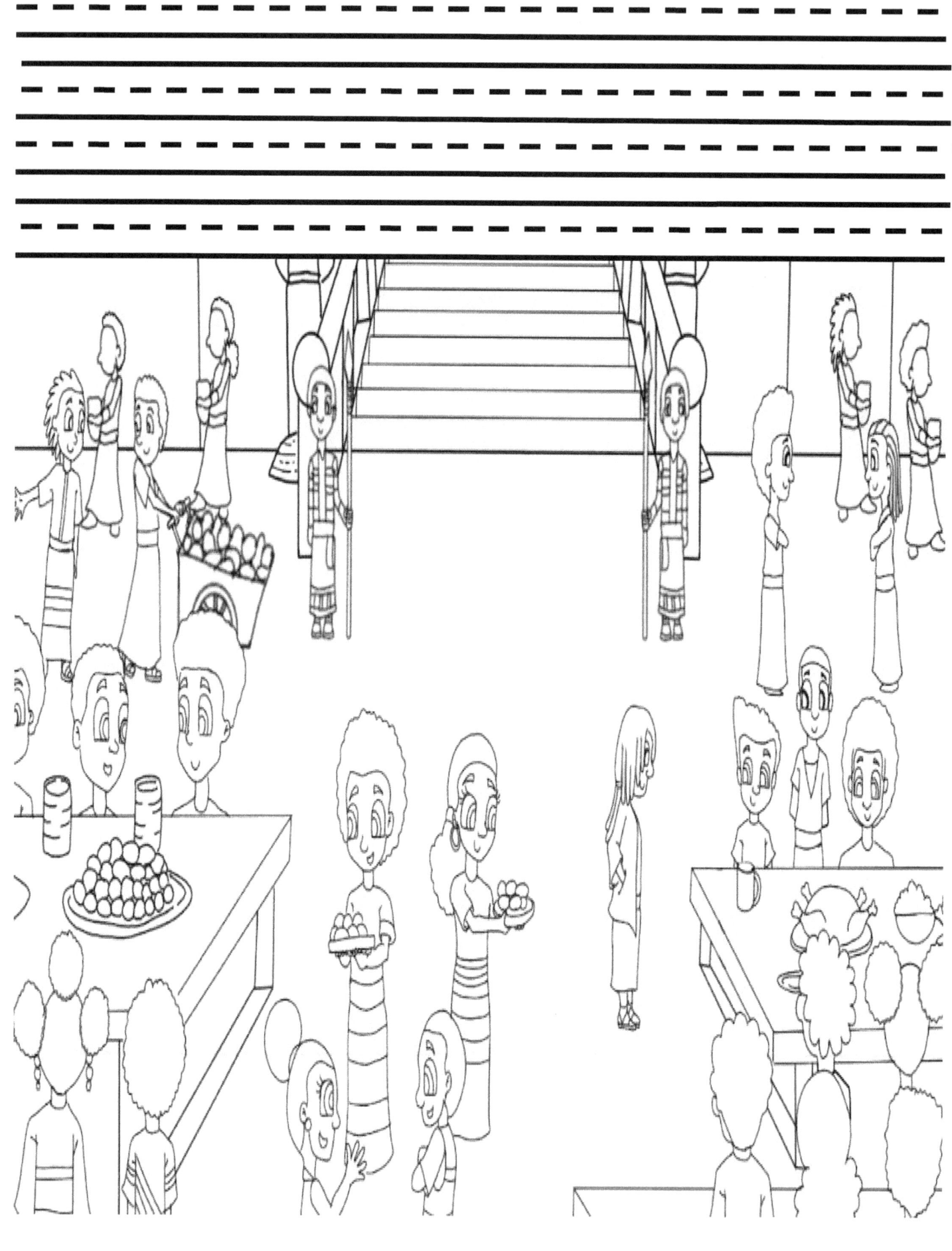

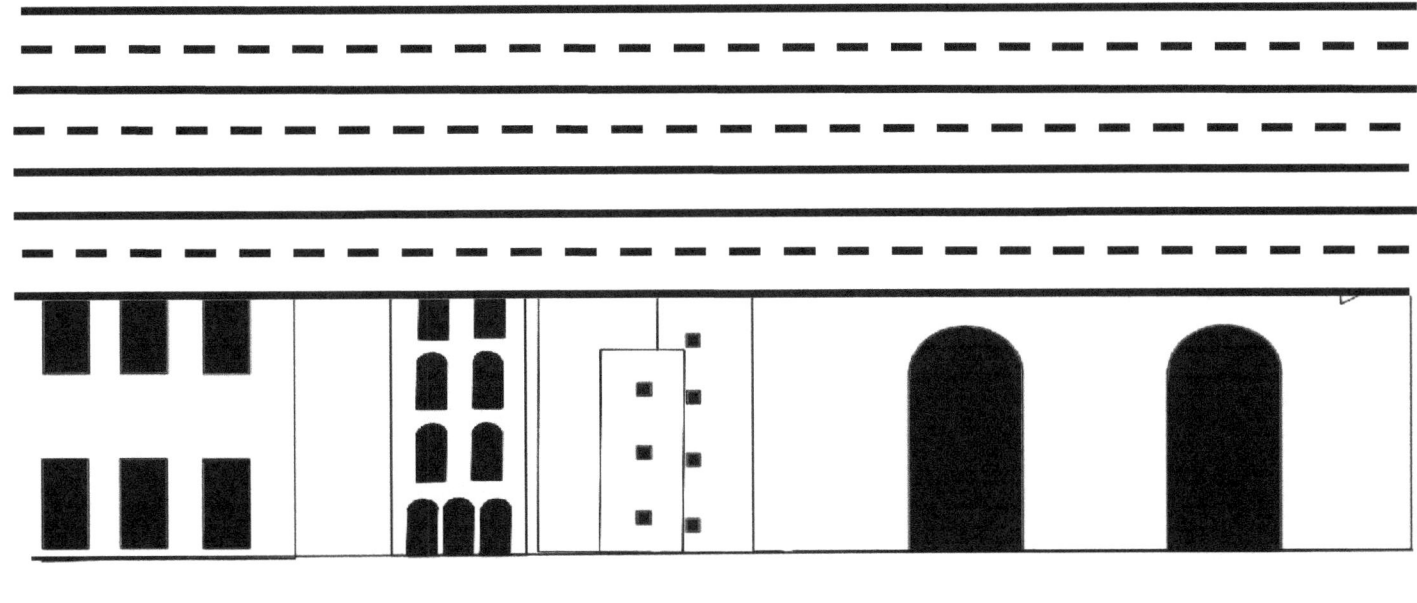

Prayer Box

HEBREW TRACING PRACTICE

Just like in the English language, the best way to get better at writing is to practice! The same goes for when you're learning Hebrew; this next section is all about practicing your Hebrew. Don't let it stress you out, make it fun, trace a couple of letters at a time, don't try to do all the letters at once. Remember slow and steady wins the race!

If you start to feel a little stressed, stop and color the tracing page instead. I created the pages in such a way that the tracing sheets double as coloring pages as well. I want you to have fun as you enjoy learning how to write in Hebrew.

One very important thing to remember is that when writing in Hebrew, you always write right to left. Whereas when you write in English, you write left to right. Start at the darkened letter and then trace over the light letters.

Parents

If you scan and print or cut out the tracing sheets, you can laminate them and use them over and over again, until your child can write each letter fluently.

ALEPH

The letter Aleph is the first letter in the Hebrew aleph-bet.

it represents oneness and unity.

א

BET

The letter Bet is the second letter in the Hebrew aleph-bet and the first letter of the Hebrew Bible.

בּ

The Bet makes the "B," sound, but sometimes, if it doesn't have a dot (called a "dagesh in Hebrew) in the middle, it then becomes the Hebrew letter Vet and has a "V" sound.

GIMEL

The letter Gimel is the third letter in the Hebrew aleph-bet.

The English letters "C" and "G" come from Gimel.

ג

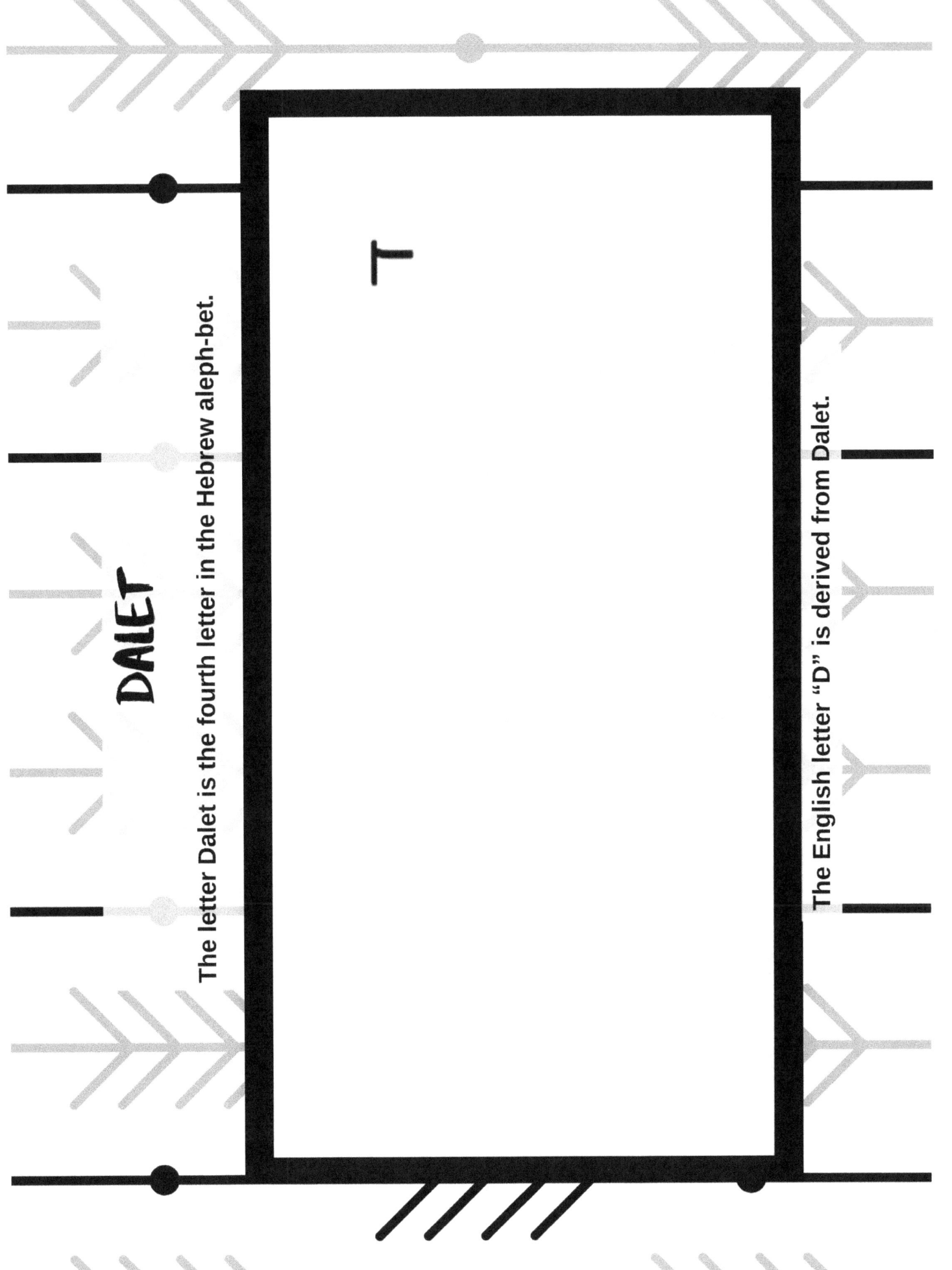

DALET

The letter Dalet is the fourth letter in the Hebrew aleph-bet.

ד

The English letter "D" is derived from Dalet.

HEI

ה

The letter Hei is the fifth letter in the Hebrew aleph-bet.

The letter Hei is the modern letter "E" in the English and Latin alphabets.

VAV

The letter Vav is the sixth letter in the Hebrew aleph-bet.

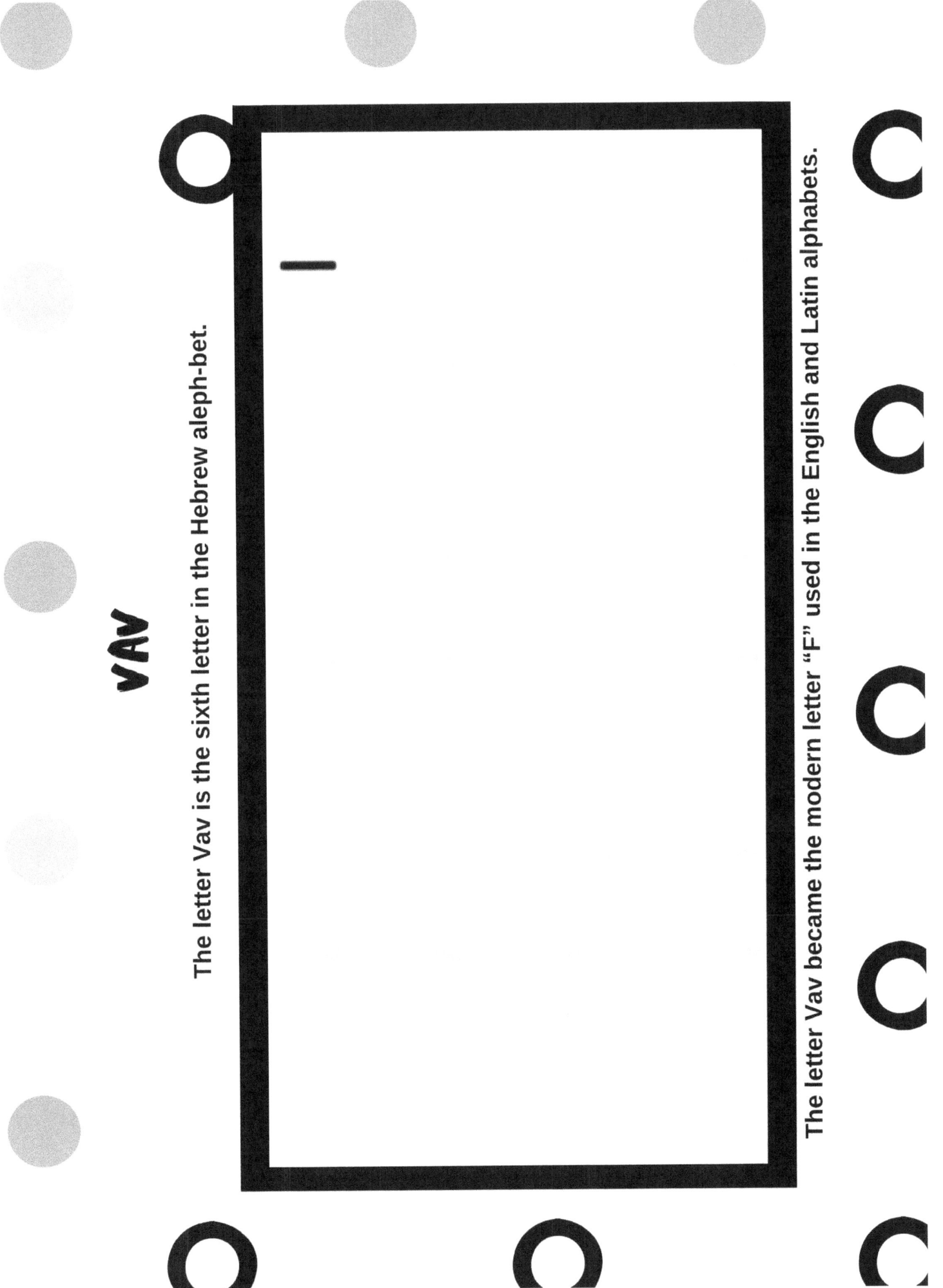

The letter Vav became the modern letter "F" used in the English and Latin alphabets.

ZAYIN

The letter Zayin is the seventh letter in the Hebrew aleph-bet.

The original meaning of the letter Zayin is a "sword" or "sharp weapon,"

ㄒ

HET

The letter Het is the eighth letter in the Hebrew aleph-bet.

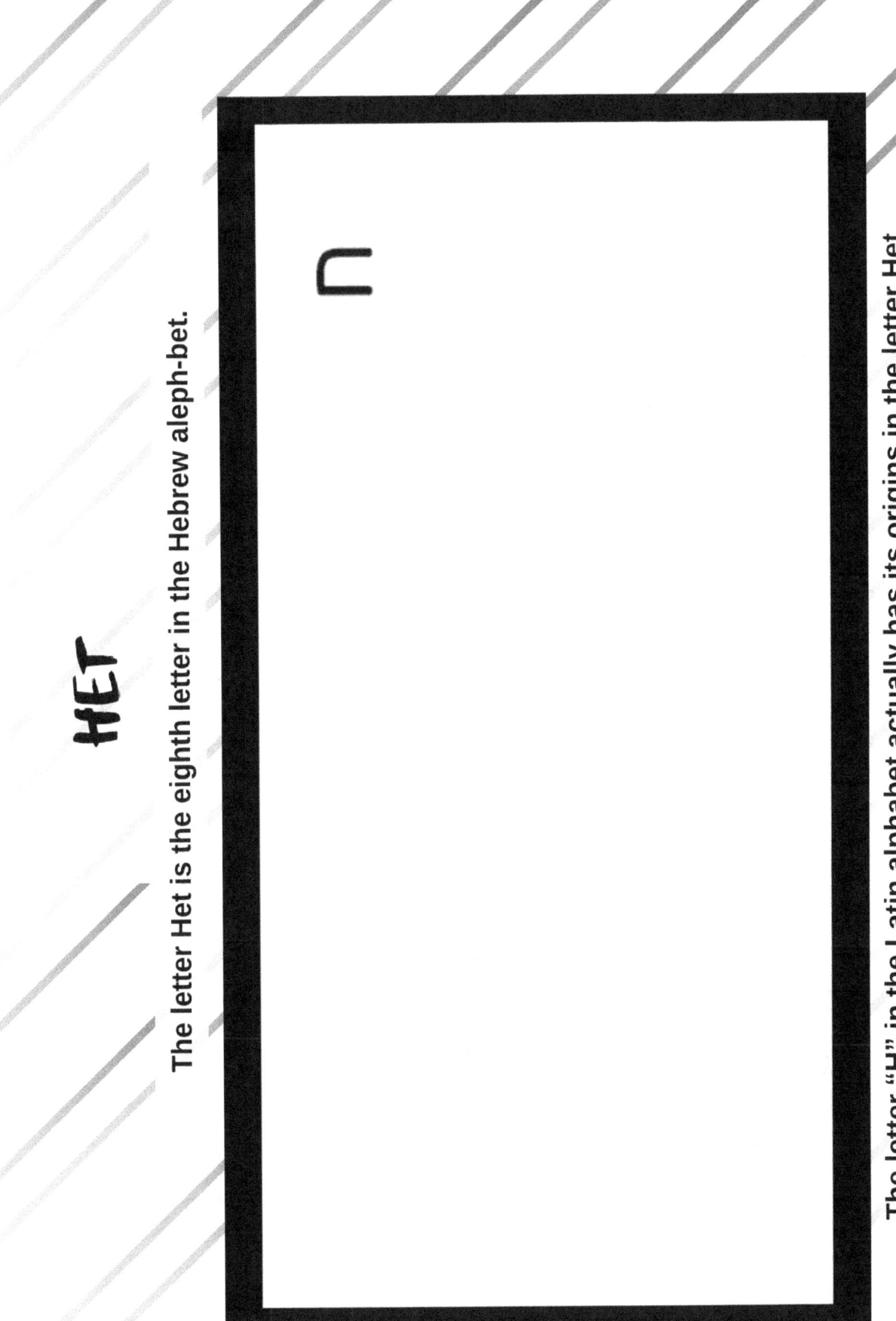

The letter "H" in the Latin alphabet actually has its origins in the letter Het.

The letter Tet is the ninth letter in the Hebrew aleph-bet.

Tet makes the sound of a letter "t."

ט

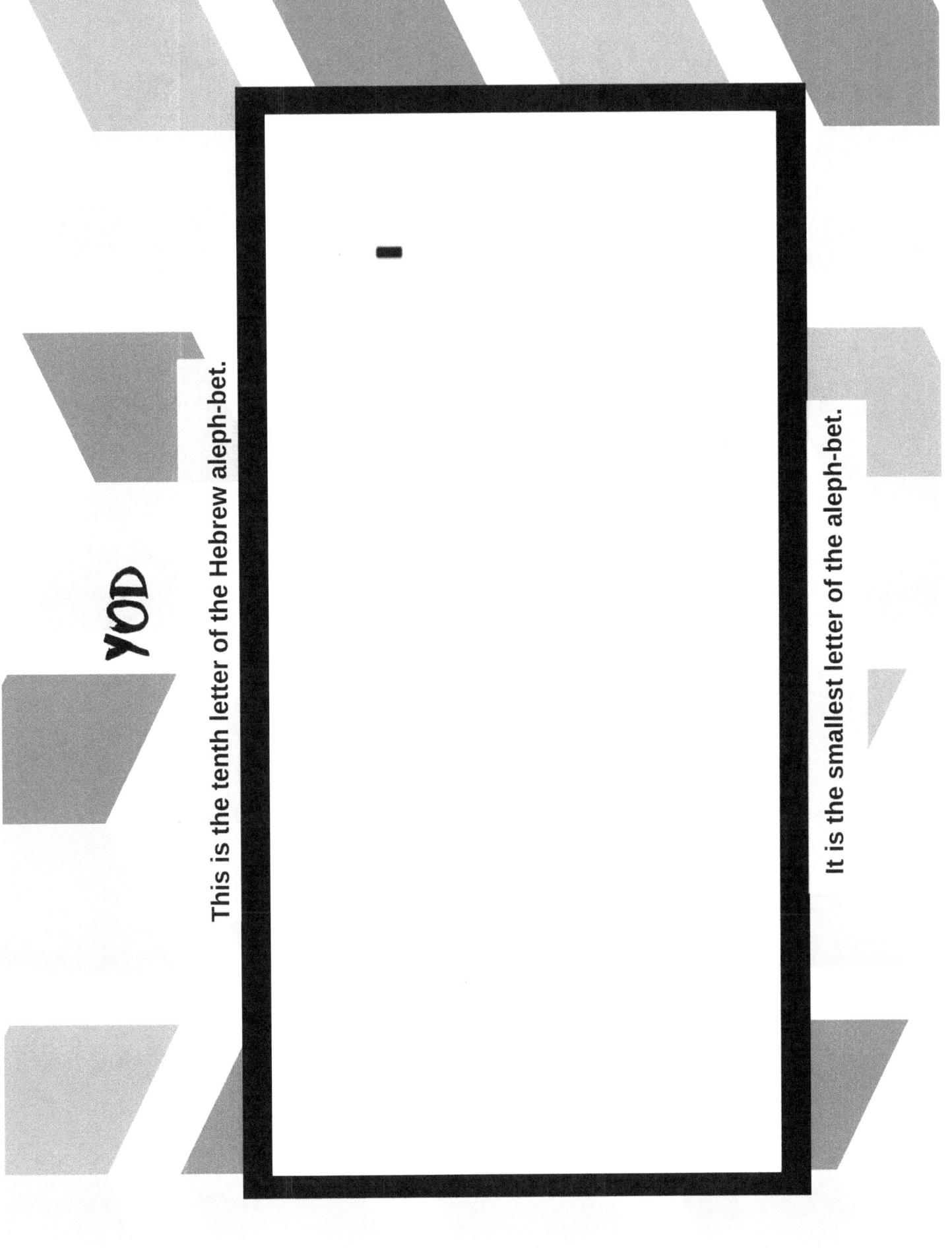

YOD

This is the tenth letter of the Hebrew aleph-bet.

It is the smallest letter of the aleph-bet.

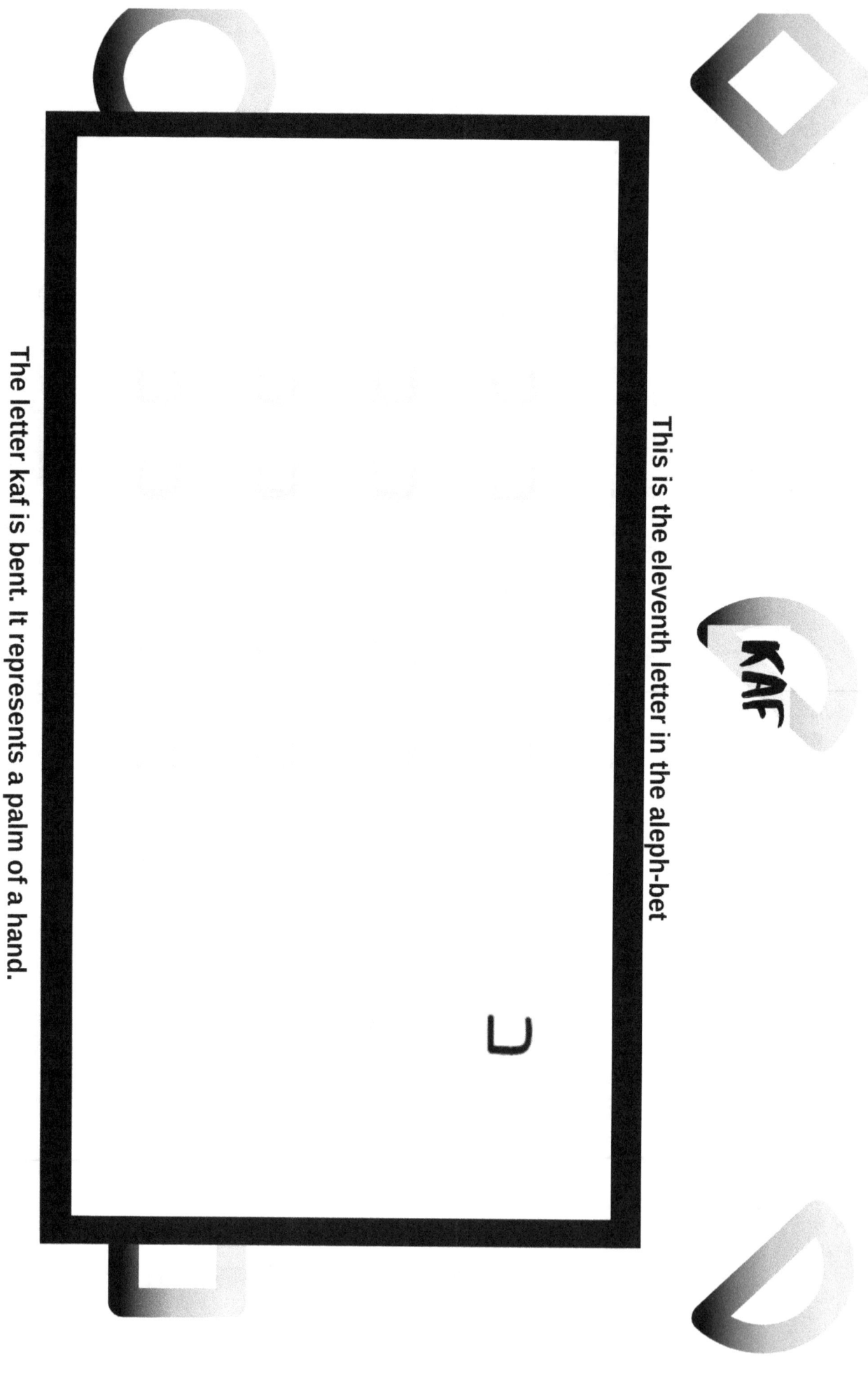

This is the eleventh letter in the aleph-bet

The letter kaf is bent. It represents a palm of a hand.

KAF

LAMED

This letter is the tallest letter of the Hebrew aleph bet.

ל

Because it is taller than all the other letters,
it represents royalty. It also represents the King of all kings, the Almighty.

This letter is written in two different ways the regular letter מ and the special final letter ם.

MEM

מ

This letter ם is closed on all sides, except for a small opening on the bottom.

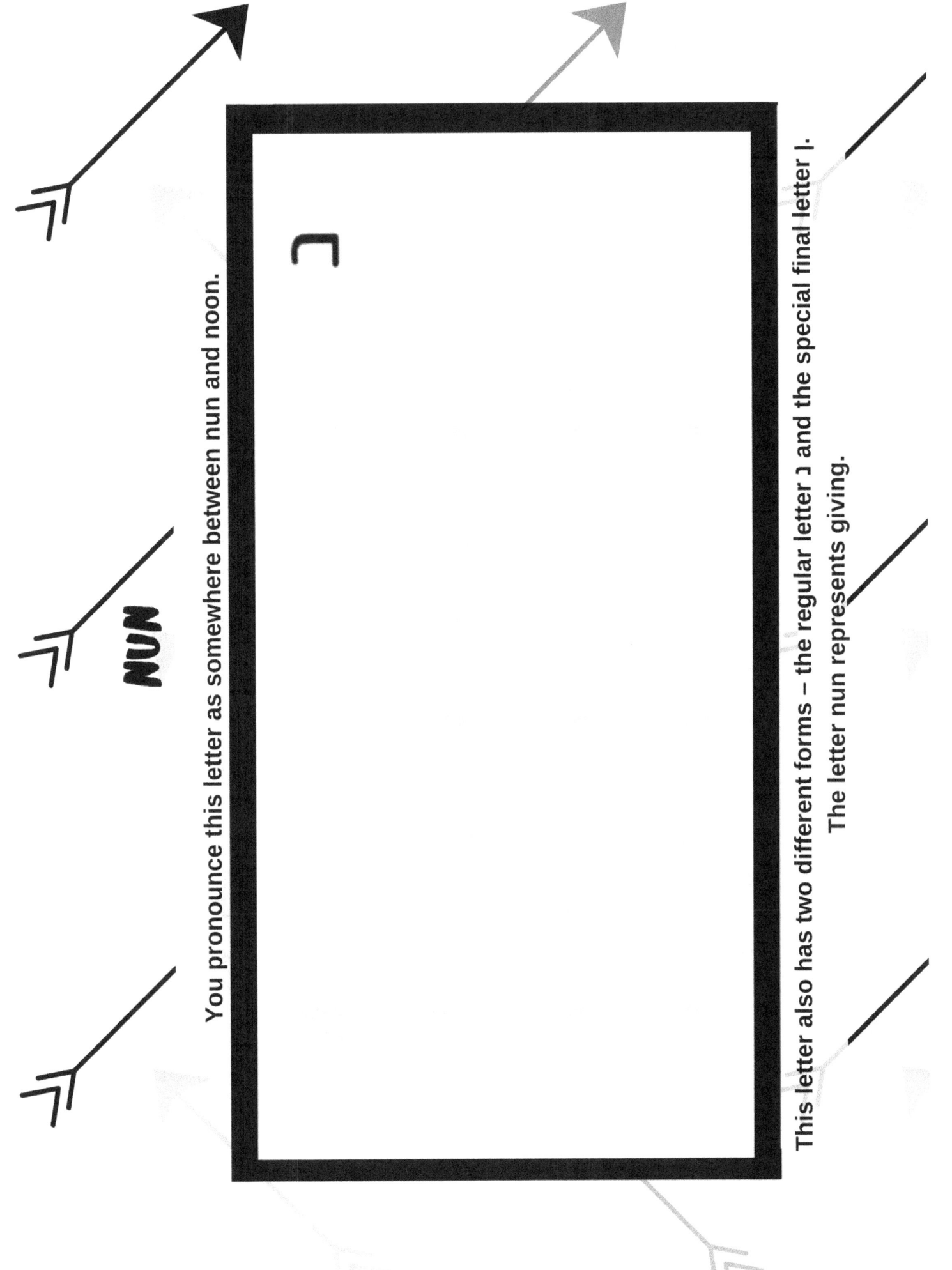

NUN

You pronounce this letter as somewhere between nun and noon.

This letter also has two different forms – the regular letter נ and the special final letter ן.
The letter nun represents giving.

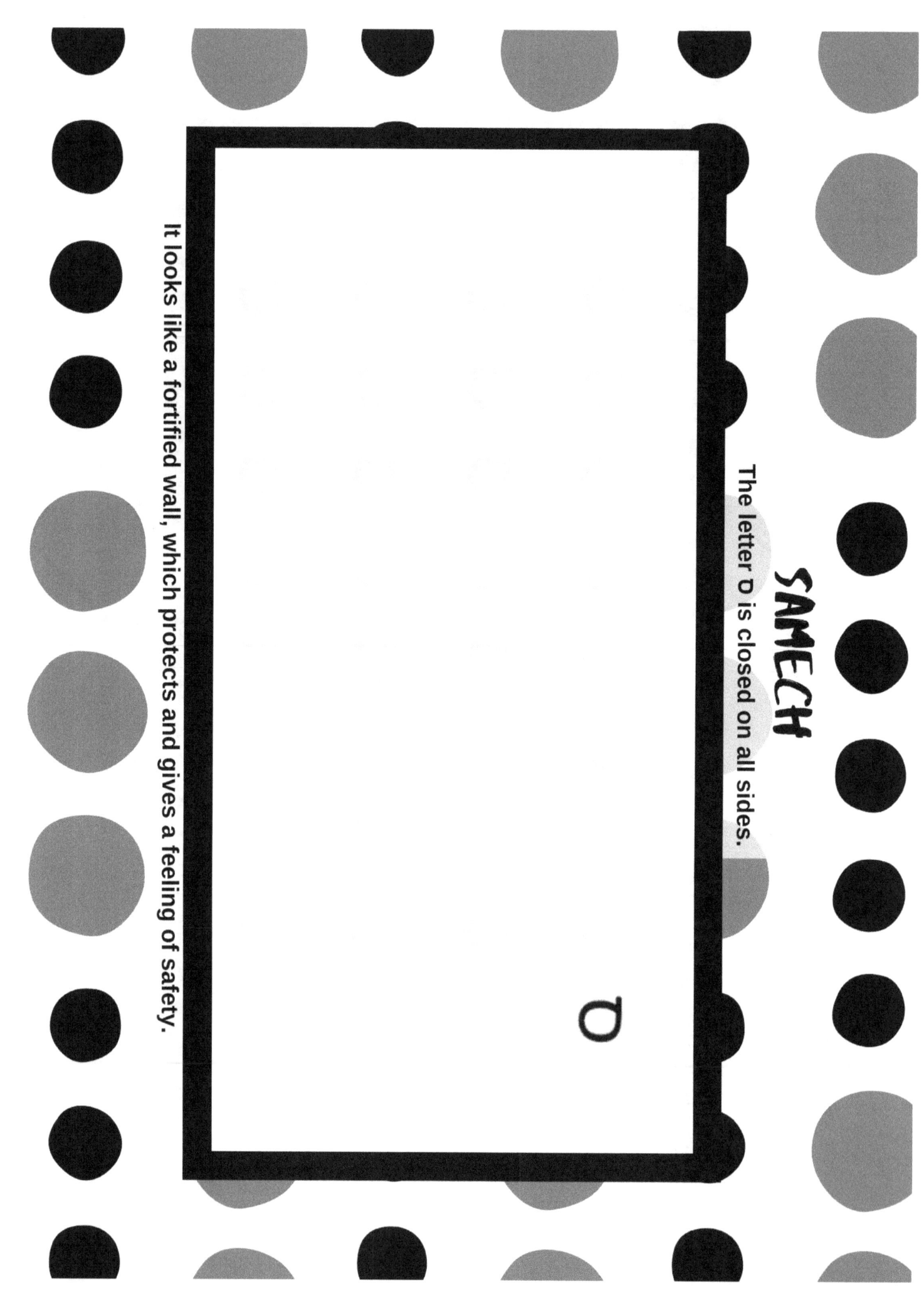

SAMECH

The letter ס is closed on all sides.

It looks like a fortified wall, which protects and gives a feeling of safety.

ס

AYIN

The Hebrew word for eye is ayin.

ע

It symbolizes the world of sight.

The word peh means mouth.

PEH

The letter peh comes after the letter ayin to teach us the order of things in life. First, the eye (ayin) sees then the mouth (peh) can start to express what the eye has seen.

TZADI

This is the eighteenth letter of the Hebrew aleph-bet.

צ

Many people mistakenly call this letter tzadik.

KUF

(Also spelled qoph) is the nineteenth letter of the aleph-bet. It makes the "k" sound.

Its numerical value is 100 it represents holiness.

ק

RESH

This is the twentieth letter in the Hebrew aleph-bet.

The letter resh represents wickedness. The order of the Hebrew letters is important and has significance.

The first letter of the word shalom peace is shin.

its sound is "SH" with a dot over the right side, and "S" with a dot over the left.

TAV

The twenty-second and final letter of the aleph-bet.

This letter symbolizes doing things with a goal in mind.

Can you find the 10 changes?

Name: _____

Meshach House of Faith

F	M	X	S	A	F	E	O	J	V	Y	P
U	F	F	R	I	E	N	D	S	P	T	X
N	P	F	W	S	G	I	R	L	T	P	B
P	L	A	F	W	V	Y	F	J	I	M	J
I	A	I	D	O	I	Y	Z	C	Y	H	F
J	Y	T	B	L	F	B	L	O	W	W	E
K	N	H	B	F	K	H	W	R	C	H	K
K	J	P	P	D	G	I	B	O	Y	Z	Z

Find the following words in the puzzle.
Words are hidden → and ↓.

BLOW	FUN	WOLF
BOY	GIRL	
FAITH	PLAY	
FRIEND	SAFE	

Abednego House of Charity

```
L  S  H  K  K  B  K  J  G  W  Q  F
S  T  E  U  C  S  I  J  Z  Z  X  I
H  R  L  W  M  T  N  J  K  V  J  R
A  O  P  L  W  A  D  W  E  R  F  E
R  N  A  O  J  N  J  K  C  I  W  F
E  G  M  V  R  D  O  D  F  R  C  E
I  A  C  E  V  V  U  H  C  S  Y  R
T  J  N  B  C  H  A  R  I  T  Y  V
```

Find the following words in the puzzle.
Words are hidden → and ↓ .

CHARITY	KIND	STAND
FIRE	LOVE	STRONG
HELP	SHARE	

Name: _____

Shadrach House of Knowledge

```
L  H  S  B  R  O  T  H  E  R  T  A
G  U  M  E  Q  L  R  Z  B  C  R  Q
D  M  A  K  Y  J  M  S  O  O  E  S
C  V  R  T  K  U  N  O  P  A  G
Y  C  T  S  H  U  T  M  K  E  D  P
S  K  J  M  R  U  N  J  S  N  G  J
D  S  A  V  E  I  Q  C  C  F  Z  X
Q  E  X  S  L  E  A  R  N  V  U  C
```

Find the following words in the puzzle.
Words are hidden → and ↓ .

BOOKS	READ	SMART
BROTHER	RUN	
LEARN	SAVE	
OPEN	SHUT	

Dots & Boxes

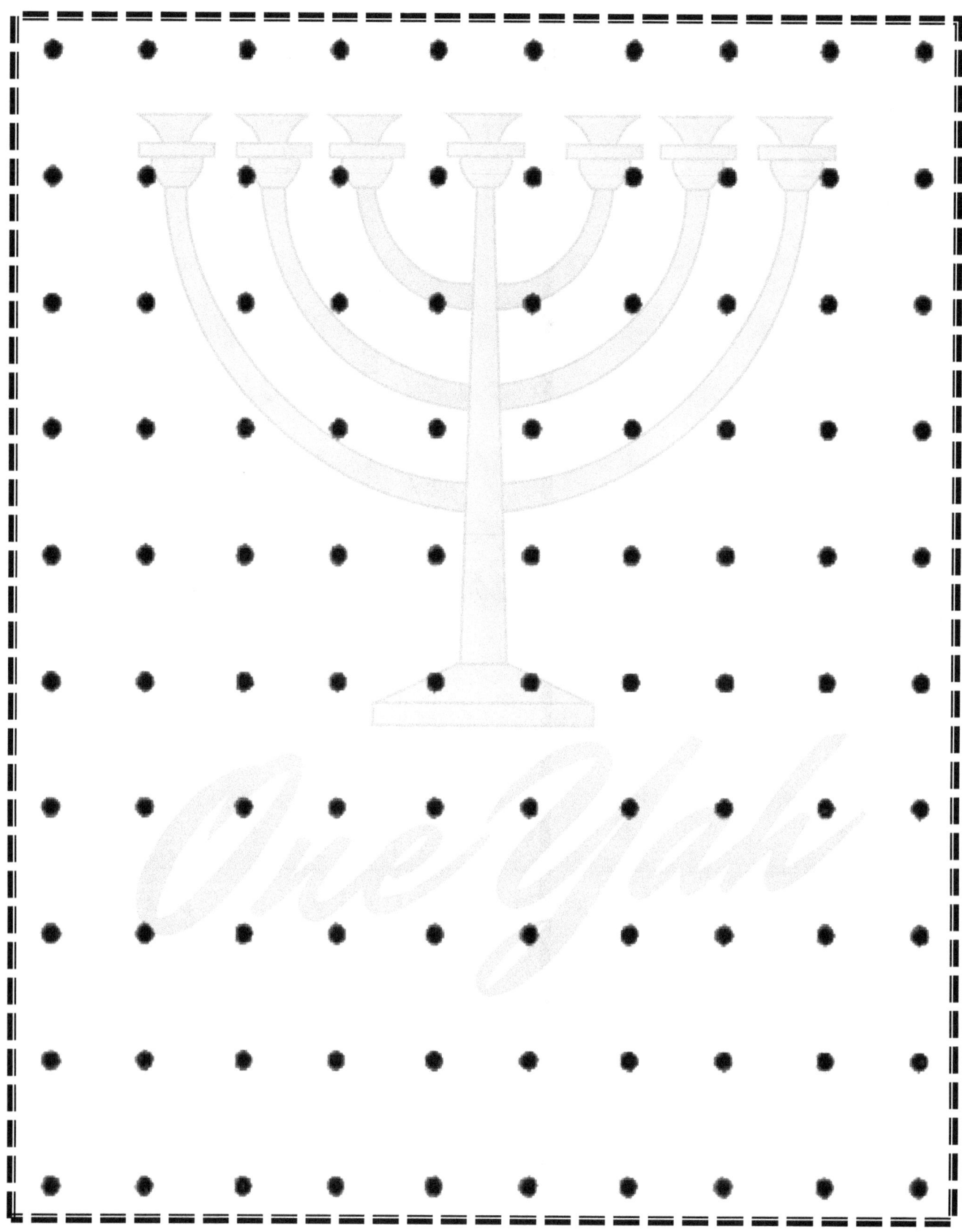

TIC TAC TOE

Holy Bible

Can you find your way to righteousness?

FINISH THE MENORAH

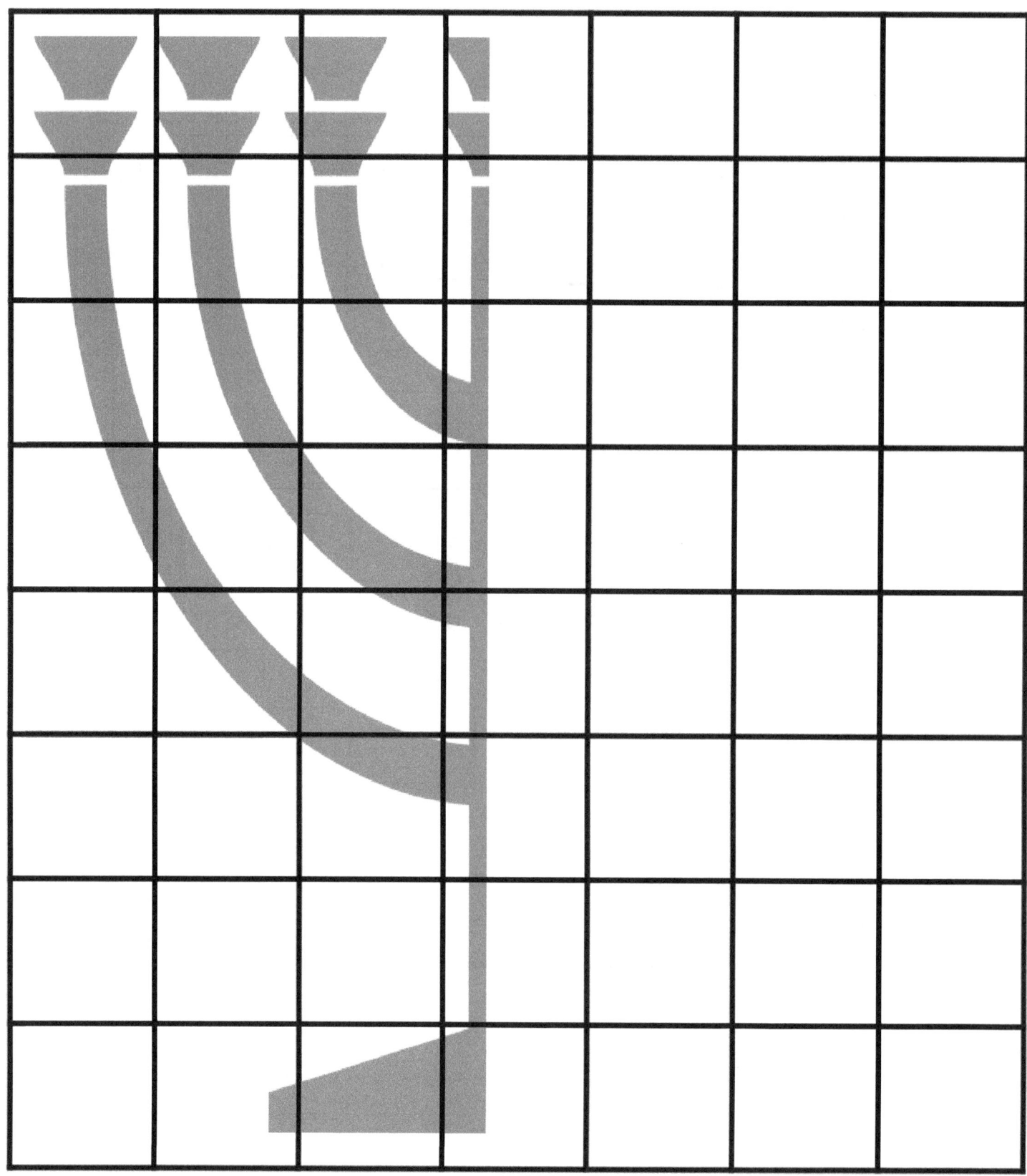